Farmyard Tales Christmas

Heather Amery
Illustrated by Stephen Cartwright
Edited by Jenny Tyler

There is a little yellow duck to find on every double page.

It's Christmas Eve at Apple Tree Farm.
Mr. and Mrs. Boot and their children,
Poppy and Sam, are getting ready
for the big day.

There's lots to do for everyone,
including Ted who works on the farm.
Poppy and Sam are getting really
excited waiting for Santa to come.

Poppy has a new kitten called Ginger.
Naughty Ginger is hiding somewhere
in every picture. Poppy can't see him
but maybe you can.

Poppy and Sam have helped Ted feed all the animals and tuck them up for the night.

Let's go home.

I'm cold.

Wait for me.

Now everyone is busy in the farmhouse.

They are all getting ready for Christmas Day.

Poppy and Sam write
letters to Santa.

Where does
Santa live?

Poppy and Sam run downstairs with their letters.

Poppy and Sam put on their coats and boots...

...and go outside.

Mr. Boot and Farmer Dray carry the tree inside.

It's bedtime for Poppy and Sam.

Very early, on Christmas morning, Poppy and Sam tiptoe downstairs.

Did Santa come?

Poppy and Sam creep
up to the tree.

Mr. and Mrs. Boot come downstairs.

Merry Christmas.

What's that behind the curtain?